AF 153867

Robert Bloomfield

The Farmer's Boy

SALZWASSER
VERLAG

Robert Bloomfield

The Farmer's Boy

Reprint of the original, first published in 1858.

1st Edition 2023 | ISBN: 978-3-37514-952-9

Verlag (Publisher): Salzwasser Verlag GmbH, Zeilweg 44, 60439 Frankfurt, Deutschland
Vertretungsberechtigt (Authorized to represent): E. Roepke, Zeilweg 44, 60439 Frankfurt, Deutschland
Druck (Print): Books on Demand GmbH, In de Tarpen 42, 22848 Norderstedt, Deutschland

THE
FARMER'S BOY.

BY

ROBERT BLOOMFIELD.

Illustrated with Thirty Engravings,
From Drawings by Birket Foster, Harrison Weir,
and G. E. Hicks.

LONDON:

SAMPSON LOW, SON & CO. 47, LUDGATE HILL.

MDCCCLVIII.

LIST OF ILLUSTRATIONS.

SPRING.

INVOCATION, ETC.—SEED TIME—HARROWING—MORNING WALKS—MILKING—
THE DAIRY—SUFFOLK CHEESE—SPRING COMING FORTH—SHEEP FOND OF
CHANGING—LAMBS AT PLAY—THE BUTCHER, ETC.

O COME, blest Spirit! whatsoe'er thou art,
Thou kindling warmth that hover'st round my heart,
Sweet inmate, hail! thou source of sterling joy,
That poverty itself cannot destroy,

B

Be thou my Muse; and, faithful still to me,
Retrace the paths of wild obscurity.
No deeds of arms my humble lines rehearse;
No Alpine wonders thunder through my verse,
The roaring cataract, the snow-topt hill,
Inspiring awe, till breath itself stands still:
Nature's sublimer scenes ne'er charm'd mine eyes,
Nor Science led me through the boundless skies;
From meaner objects far my raptures flow;
O point these raptures! bid my bosom glow!
And lead my soul to ecstasies of praise
For all the blessings of my infant days!
Bear me through regions where gay Fancy dwells;
But mould to Truth's fair form what Memory tells.

Live, trifling incidents, and grace my song,
That to the humblest menial belong:
To him whose drudgery unheeded goes,
His joys unreckon'd as his cares or woes;
Though joys and cares in every path are sown,
And youthful minds have feelings of their own,
Quick-springing sorrows, transient as the dew,
Delights from trifles, trifles ever new.
'Twas thus with Giles: meek, fatherless, and poor:
Labour his portion, but he felt no more;
No stripes, no tyranny his steps pursued;
His life was constant, cheerful servitude:
Strange to the world, he wore a bashful look,
The fields his study, Nature was his book;
And, as revolving Seasons changed the scene
From heat to cold, tempestuous to serene,
Though every change still varied his employ,
Yet each new duty brought its share of joy.

Where noble Grafton spreads his rich domains,
Round Euston's water'd vale, and sloping plains,

Where woods and groves in solemn grandeur rise,
Where the kite brooding unmolested flies;
The woodcock and the painted pheasant race,
And skulking foxes, destined for the chace;

There Giles, untaught and unrepining, stray'd
Through every copse, and grove, and winding glade;
There his first thoughts to Nature's charms inclined,
That stamps devotion on th' inquiring mind.

A little farm his generous Master till'd,
Who with peculiar grace his station fill'd ;
By deeds of hospitality endear'd,
Served from affection, for his worth revered ;
A happy offspring blest his plenteous board,
His fields were fruitful, and his barns well stored,
And fourscore ewes he fed ; a sturdy team ;
And lowing kine that grazed beside the stream :
Unceasing industry he kept in view;
And never lack'd a job for Giles to do.

Fled now the sullen murmurs of the North,
The splendid raiment of the Spring peeps forth ;
Her universal green, and the clear sky,
Delight still more and more the gazing eye.
Wide o'er the fields, in rising moisture strong,
Shoots up the simple flower, or creeps along
The mellow'd soil ; imbibing fairer hues,
Or sweets from frequent showers and evening dews ;
That summon from their sheds the slumb'ring ploughs,
While health impregnates every breeze that blows.
No wheels support the diving, pointed share ;
No groaning ox is doom'd to labour there ;
No helpmates teach the docile steed his road ;
(Alike unknown the plough-boy and the goad ;)
But, unassisted through each toilsome day,
With smiling brow the ploughman cleaves his way,
Draws his fresh parallels, and, wid'ning still,
Treads slow the heavy dale, or climbs the hill :
Strong on the wing his busy followers play,
Where writhing earth-worms meet th' unwelcome day ;
Till all is changed, and hill and level down
Assume a livery of sober brown ;
Again disturb'd, when Giles with wearying strides
'From ridge to ridge the ponderous harrow guides :
His heels deep sinking every step he goes,

Till dirt adhesive loads his clouted shoes.
Welcome, green headland! firm beneath his feet;
Welcome, the friendly bank's refreshing seat;
There, warm with toil, his panting horses browse
Their shelt'ring canopy of pendent boughs;

Till rest, delicious, chase each transient pain,
And new-born vigour swell in every vein.
Hour after hour, and day to day succeeds;
Till every clod and deep-drawn furrow spreads
To crumbling mould; a level surface clear,

And strew'd with corn to crown the rising year;
And o'er the whole Giles, once transverse again,
In earth's moist bosom buries up the grain.
The work is done; no more to man is given;
The grateful Farmer trusts the rest to Heaven.
Yet oft with anxious heart he looks around,
And marks the first green blade that breaks the ground;
In fancy sees his trembling oats uprun,
His tufted barley yellow with the sun;
Sees clouds propitious shed their timely store,
And all his harvest gather'd round his door.
But still unsafe the big swoln grain below,
A fav'rite morsel with the rook and crow;
From field to field the flock increasing goes;
To level crops most formidable foes:
Their danger well the wary plunderers know,
And place a watch on some conspicuous bough;
Yet oft the skulking gunner by surprise
Will scatter death amongst them as they rise.
These, hung in triumph round the spacious field,
At best will but a short-lived terror yield:
Nor guards of property: (not penal law,
But harmless riflemen of rags and straw;)
Familiarised to these, they boldly rove,
Nor heed such sentinels that never move.
Let then your birds lie prostrate on the earth,
In dying posture, and with wings stretcht forth!
Shift them at eve or morn from place to place,
And Death shall terrify the pilfering race;
In the mid air, while circling round and round,
They call their lifeless comrades from the ground;
With quick'ning wing and notes of loud alarm,
Warn the whole flock to shun th' impending harm.

This task had Giles, in fields remote from home;
Oft has he wish'd the rosy morn to come:

Yet never famed. was he nor foremost found
To break the seal of sleep; his sleep was sound :
But when at day-break summon'd from his bed,
Light as the lark that carol'd o'er his head.—

His sandy way, deep-worn by hasty showers,
O'er-arch'd with oaks that form'd fantastic bow'rs,
Waving aloft their tow'ring branches proud,
In borrow'd tinges from the eastern cloud,

And sitting hens, for constant war prepared;
A concert strange to that which late he heard.
Straight to the meadow then he whistling goes;
With well-known halloo calls his lazy cows:
Down the rich pasture heedlessly they graze,
Or hear the summons with an idle gaze;

For well they know the cow-yard yields no more
Its tempting fragrance, nor its wintry store.
Reluctance marks their steps, sedate and slow;
The right of conquest all the law they know;
The strong press on, the weak by turns succeed,
And one superior always takes the lead;

C

Is ever foremost, wheresoe'er they stray;
Allow'd precedence, 'undisputed sway;
With jealous pride her station is maintain'd,
For many a broil that post of honour gain'd.
At home, the yard affords a grateful scene;
For Spring makes e'en a miry cow-yard clean.
Thence from its chalky bed behold convey'd
The rich manure that drenching Winter made,
Which piled near home, grows green with many a weed,
A promised nutriment for Autumn's seed.
Forth comes the Maid, and like the morning smiles;
The Mistress too, and follow'd close by Giles.
A friendly tripod forms their humble seat,
With pales bright scour'd, and delicately sweet.
Where shadowing elms obstruct the morning ray,
Begins the work, begins the simple lay;
The full-charged udder yields its willing streams,
While Mary sings some lover's amorous dreams;
And crouching Giles beneath a neighbouring tree
Tugs o'er his pail, and chants with equal glee;
Whose hat with tatter'd brim, of nap so bare,
From the cow's side purloins a coat of hair,
A mottled ensign of his harmless trade,
An unambitious, peaceable cockade.
As unambitious too that cheerful aid
The Mistress yields beside her rosy Maid;
With joy she views her plenteous reeking store,
And bears a brimmer to the dairy door;
Her cows dismiss'd, the luscious mead to roam,
Till eve again recal them loaded home.
And now the Dairy claims her choicest care,
And half her household find employment there:
Slow rolls the churn, its load of clogging cream
At once foregoes its quality and name:
From knotty particles first floating wide,
Congealing butter's dash'd from side to side;

Streams of new milk through flowing coolers stray,
And snow-white curd abounds, and wholesome whey.
Due north th' unglazed windows, cold and clear,

For warming sunbeams are unwelcome here.
Brisk goes the work beneath each busy hand,
And Giles must trudge, whoever gives command ;

A Gibeonite that serves them all by turns :
He drains the pump, from him the fagot burns ;
From him the noisy hogs demand their food ;
While at his heels run many a chirping brood,
Or down his path in expectation stand,
With equal claims upon his strewing hand.
Thus wastes the morn, till each with pleasure sees
The bustle o'er, and press'd the new-made cheese.

Unrivall'd stands thy country Cheese, O Giles !
Whose very name alone engenders smiles ;
Whose fame abroad by every tongue is spoke,
The well-known butt of many a flinty joke,
That pass like current coin the nation through ;
And, ah ! experience proves the satire true.
Provision's grave, thou ever-craving mart,
Dependent, huge Metropolis ! where Art
Her poring thousands stows in breathless rooms,
'Midst pois'nous smokes, and steams, and rattling looms :
Where Grandeur revels in unbounded stores ;
Restraint, a slighted stranger at their doors !
Thou, like a whirlpool, drain'st the countries round,
Till London market, London price, resound
Through every town, round every passing load,
And dairy produce throngs the eastern road :
Delicious veal and butter, every hour,
From Essex lowlands, and the banks of Stour ;
And further far, where numerous herds repose,
From Orwell's brink, from Waveny, or Ouse.
Hence Suffolk dairy-wives run mad for cream,
And leave their milk with nothing but its name ;
Its name derision and reproach pursue,
And strangers tell of "three times skimm'd sky-blue."
To cheese converted, what can be its boast ?
What, but the common virtues of a post !
If drought o'ertake it faster than the knife,

Most fair it bids for stubborn length of life,
And, like the oaken shelf whereon 'tis laid,
Mocks the weak efforts of the bending blade ;
Or in the hog-trough rests in perfect spite,
Too big to swallow, and too hard to bite.

Inglorious victory ! Ye Cheshire meads,
Or Severn's flow'ry dales, where Plenty treads,
Was your rich milk to suffer wrongs like these,
Farewell your pride ! farewell, renowned cheese !

The skimmer dread, whose ravages alone
Thus turn the meads' sweet nectar into stone.

Neglected now the early daisy lies ;
Nor thou, pale primrose, bloom'st the only prize :
Advancing Spring profusely spreads abroad
Flow'rs of all hues, with sweetest fragrance stored ;
Where'er she treads Love gladdens every plain,
Delight on tiptoe bears her lucid train ;
Sweet Hope with conscious brow before her flies,
Anticipating wealth from Summer skies ;
All Nature feels her renovating sway ;
The sheep-fed pasture, and the meadow gay ;
And trees and shrubs, no longer budding seen,
Display the new-grown branch of lighter green ;
On airy downs the idling shepherd lies,
And sees to-morrow in the marbled skies.
Here then, my soul, thy darling theme pursue,
For every day was Giles a shepherd too.

Small was his charge : no wilds had they to roam ;
But bright enclosures circling round their home.
No yellow-blossom'd furze, nor stubborn thorn,
The heath's rough produce, had their fleeces torn ;
Yet ever roving, ever seeking thee,
Enchanting spirit, dear Variety !
O happy tenants, prisoners of a day !
Released to ease, to pleasure, and to play ;
Indulged through every field by turns to range,
And taste them all in one continual change.
For though luxuriant their grassy food,
Sheep long confined but loathe the present good :
Bleating around the homeward gate they meet,
And starve, and pine, with plenty at their feet.
Loosed from the winding lane, a joyful throng,
See, o'er yon pasture, how they pour along !

Giles round their boundaries takes his usual stroll ;
Sees every pass secured, and fences whole ;
High fences, proud to charm the gazing eye,

Where many a nestling first essays to fly ;
Where blows the woodbine, faintly streak'd with red,
And rests on every bough its tender head ;

Round the young ash its twining branches meet,
Or crown the hawthorn with its odour sweet.

Say, ye that know, ye who have felt and seen,
Spring's morning smiles, and soul-enliv'ning green,
Say, did you give the thrilling transport way?
Did your eye brighten, when young lambs at play
Leap'd o'er your path with animated pride,
Or gazed in merry clusters by your side?
Ye who can smile, to wisdom no disgrace,
At the arch meaning of a kitten's face:
If spotless innocence, and infant mirth,
Excites to praise, or gives reflection birth;
In shades like these pursue your fav'rite joy,
'Midst Nature's revels, sports that never cloy.

A few begin a short but vigorous race,
And Indolence abash'd soon flies the place;
Thus challenged forth, see thither one by one,
From every side assembling playmates run;
A thousand wily antics mark their stay,
A starting crowd, impatient of delay.
Like the fond dove from fearful prison freed,
Each seems to say, "Come, let us try our speed;"
Away they scour, impetuous, ardent, strong,
The green turf trembling as they bound along;
Adown the slope, then up the hillock climb,
Where every molehill is a bed of thyme;
There panting stop; yet scarcely can refrain;
A bird, a leaf will set them off again;
Or, if a gale with strength unusual blow,
Scatt'ring the wild-brier roses into snow,
Their little limbs increasing efforts try,
Like the torn flow'r the fair assemblage fly.
Ah, fallen rose! sad emblem of their doom;
Frail as thyself, they perish as they bloom!

Though unoffending Innocence may plead,
Though frantic ewes may mourn the savage deed,
Their shepherd comes, a messenger of blood,
And drives them bleating from their sports and food.
Care loads his brow, and pity wrings his heart,
For lo, the murd'ring butcher, with his cart,
Demands the firstlings of his flock to die,
And makes a sport of life and liberty!
His gay companions Giles beholds no more;
Closed are their eyes, their fleeces drench'd in gore;
Nor can compassion, with her softest notes,
Withhold the knife that plunges through their throats.

Down, indignation! hence, ideas foul!
Away the shocking image from my soul!
Let kindlier visitants attend my way,
Beneath the approaching Summer's fervid ray;
Nor thankless glooms obtrude, nor cares annoy,
Whilst the sweet theme is universal joy.

D

SUMMER.

TURNIP SOWING—WHEAT RIPENING—SPARROWS—INSECTS—THE SKYLARK—
REAPING, ETC.—HARVEST FIELD, DAIRY-MAID, ETC.—LABOURS OF THE
BARN—THE GANDER—NIGHT—A THUNDER-STORM—HARVEST-HOME—
REFLECTIONS, ETC.

The Farmer's life displays in every part
A moral lesson to the sensual heart.
Though in the lap of Plenty, thoughtful still,
He looks beyond the present good or ill;

Nor estimates alone one blessing's worth,
From changeful seasons, or capricious earth,
But views the future with the present hours,
And looks for failures as he looks for showers;
For casual as for certain want prepares,
And round his yard the reeking haystack rears;
Or clover, blossom'd lovely to the sight,
His team's rich store through many a wintry night.
What though abundance round his dwelling spreads,
Though, ever moist, his self-improving meads
Supply his dairy with a copious flood,
And seem to promise unexhausted food;
That promise fails, when buried deep in snow,
And vegetative juices cease to flow.
For this his plough turns up the destined lands,
Whence stormy Winter draws its full demands;
For this, the seed minutely small he sows,
Whence, sound and sweet, the hardy turnip grows.
But how unlike to April's closing days!
High climbs the Sun, and darts his powerful rays;
Whitens the fresh-drawn mould, and pierces through
The cumbrous clods that tumble round the plough.
O'er heaven's bright azure hence with joyful eyes
The Farmer sees dark clouds assembling rise;
Borne o'er his fields a heavy torrent falls,
And strikes the earth in hasty driving squalls.
" Right welcome down, ye precious drops," he cries;
But soon, too soon, the partial blessing flies.
" Boy, bring the harrows, try how deep the rain
Has forced its way." He comes, but comes in vain;
Dry dust beneath the bubbling surface lurks,
And mocks the pains the more, the more he works:
Still, 'midst huge clods, he plunges on forlorn,
That laugh his harrows and the shower to scorn.
E'en thus the living clod, the stubborn fool,
Resists the stormy lectures of the school,

Till tried with gentler means, the dunce to please,
His head imbibes right reason by degrees ;
As when from eve till morning's wakeful hour,
Light constant rain evinces secret pow'r,

And ere the day resumes its wonted smiles,
Presents a cheerful, easy task for Giles.
Down with a touch the mellow'd soil is laid,
And yon tall crop next claims his timely aid ;

Thither well pleased he hies, assured to find
Wild, trackless haunts, and objects to his mind.

Shot up from broad rank blades that droop below,
The nodding wheat-ear forms a graceful bow,
With milky kernels starting full, weigh'd down,
Ere yet the sun hath tinged its head with brown ;
There thousands in a flock, for ever gay,
Loud chirping sparrows welcome on the day,
And from the mazes of the leafy thorn
Drop one by one upon the bending corn.
Giles with a pole assails their close retreats,
And round the grass-grown dewy border beats ;
On either side completely overspread,
Here branches bend, there corn o'ertops his' head.
Green covert, hail ! for through the varying year
No hours so sweet, no scene to him so dear.
Here Wisdom's placid eye delighted sees
His frequent intervals of lonely ease,
And with one ray his infant soul inspires,
Just kindling there her never-dying fires,
Whence solitude derives peculiar charms,
And heaven-directed thought his bosom warms.
Just where the parting bough's light shadows play,
Scarce in the shade, nor in the scorching day,
Stretch'd on the turf he lies, a peopled bed,
Where swarming insects creep around his head.
The small dust-colour'd beetle climbs with pain,
O'er the smooth plantain-leaf, a spacious plain !
Thence higher still, by countless steps convey'd,
He gains the summit of a shiv'ring blade,
And flirts his filmy wings, and looks around,
Exulting in his distance from the ground.
The tender speckled moth here dancing seen,
The vaulting grasshopper of glossy green,
And all prolific Summer's sporting train,

Their little lives by various pow'rs sustain.
But what can unassisted vision do?
What but recoil where most it would pursue;
His patient gaze but finish with a sigh,
When Music waking speaks the skylark nigh!
Just starting from the corn, he cheerly sings,
And trusts with conscious pride his downy wings;
Still louder breathes, and in the face of day
Mounts up, and calls on Giles to mark his way.
Close to his eyes his hat he instant bends,
And forms a friendly telescope, that lends
Just aid enough to dull the glaring light,
And place the wand'ring bird before his sight,
That oft beneath a light cloud sweeps along,
Lost for a while, yet pours the varied song:
The eye still follows, and the cloud moves by,
Again he stretches up the clear blue sky;
His form, his motion, undistinguish'd quite,
Save when he wheels direct from shade to light:
E'en then the songster a mere speck became.
Gliding like fancy's bubbles in a dream,
The gazer sees; but yielding to repose,
Unwittingly his jaded eyelids close.
Delicious sleep! From sleep who could forbear,
With no more guilt than Giles, and no more care?
Peace o'er his slumbers waves her guardian wing,
Nor Conscience once disturbs him with a sting;
He wakes refresh'd from every trivial pain,
And takes his pole, and brushes round again.

Its dark-green hue, its sicklier tints all fail,
And ripening Harvest rustles in the gale.
A glorious sight, if glory dwells below,
Where Heaven's munificence makes all the show
O'er every field and golden prospect found,
That glads the Ploughman's Sunday morning's round,

When on some eminence he takes his stand,
To judge the smiling produce of the land.
Here Vanity slinks back, her head to hide :

What is there here to flatter human pride ?
The tow'ring fabric, or the dome's loud roar,
And steadfast columns, may astonish more,

Where the charm'd gazer long delighted stays,
Yet traced but to the architect the praise;
Whilst here, the veriest clown that treads the sod,
Without one scruple gives the praise to God;
And twofold joys possess his raptured mind,
From gratitude and admiration join'd.

Here, 'midst the boldest triumphs of her worth,
Nature herself invites the reapers forth;
Dares the keen sickle from its twelvemonth's rest,
And gives that ardour which in every breast,
From infancy to age, alike appears,
When the first sheaf its plumy top uprears.
No rake takes here what Heaven to all bestows—
Children of want, for you the bounty flows!
And every cottage from the plenteous store
Receives a burden nightly at his door.

Hark! where the sweeping scythe now rips along,
Each sturdy Mower, emulous and strong,
Whose writhing form meridian heat defies,
Bends o'er his work, and every sinew tries;
Prostrates the waving treasure at his feet,
But spares the rising clover, short and sweet.
Come, Health! come, Jollity! light-footed, come;
Here hold your revels, and make this your home.
Each heart awaits and hails you as its own;
Each moisten'd brow that scorns to wear a frown;
Th' unpeopled dwelling mourns its tenants stray'd;
E'en the domestic laughing dairy-maid
Hies to the field, the general toil to share.
Meanwhile the Farmer quits his elbow-chair,
His cool brick floor, his pitcher, and his ease,
And braves the sultry beams, and gladly sees
His gates thrown open, and his team abroad,
The ready group attendant on his word,

To turn the swarth, the quiv'ring load to rear,
Or ply the busy rake, the land to clear.
Summer's light garb itself now cumbrous grown,
Each his thin doublet in the shade throws down;

Where oft the mastiff skulks with half-shut eye,
And rouses at the stranger passing by;
Whilst unrestrain'd the social converse flows,
And every breast Love's powerful impulse knows,

E

And rival wits with more than rustic grace
Confess the presence of a pretty face.

For, lo! encircled there, the lovely Maid,
In youth's own bloom and native smiles array'd;
Her hat awry, divested of her gown,
Her creaking stays of leather, stout and brown;—
Invidious barrier! Why art thou so high,
When the slight covering of her neck slips by,
There half revealing to the eager sight,
Her full, ripe bosom, exquisitely white?
In many a local tale of harmless mirth,
And many a jest of momentary birth,
She bears a part, and as she stops to speak,
Strokes back the ringlets from her glowing cheek.

Now noon gone by, and four declining hours,
The weary limbs relax their boasted powers;
Thirst rages strong, the fainting spirits fail,
And ask the sov'reign cordial, home-brew'd ale:
Beneath some shelt'ring heap of yellow corn
Rests the hoop'd keg, and friendly cooling horn,
That mocks alike the goblet's brittle frame,
Its costlier potions, and its nobler name.
To Mary first the brimming draught is given,
By toil made welcome as the dews of heaven,
And never lip that press'd its homely edge
Had kinder blessings, or a heartier pledge.

Of wholesome viands here a banquet smiles,
A common cheer for all;—e'en humble Giles,
Who joys his trivial services to yield
Amidst the fragrance of the open field;
Oft doom'd in suffocating heat to bear
The cobweb'd barn's impure and dusty air;
To ride in murky state the panting steed,

Destin'd aloft th' unloaded grain to tread,
Where, in his path as heaps on heaps are thrown,
He rears, and plunges the loose mountain down:
Laborious task! with what delight, when done,
Both horse and rider greet th' unclouded sun!

Yet by th' unclouded sun are hourly bred
The bold assailants that surround thine head,
Poor, patient Ball! and with insulting wing
Roar in thine ears, and dart the piercing sting;
In thy behalf the crest-waved boughs avail
More than thy short-clipt remnant of a tail,

A moving mockery, a useless name,
A living proof of cruelty and shame.
Shame to the man, whatever fame he bore,
Who took from thee what man can ne'er restore,
Thy weapon of defence, thy chiefest good,
When swarming flies contending suck thy blood.
Nor thine alone the suff'ring, thine the care,
The fretful ewe bemoans an equal share;
Tormented into sores, her head she hides,
Or angry sweeps them from her new-shorn sides.
Penn'd in the yard, e'en now at closing day
Unruly cows with mark'd impatience stay,
And vainly striving to escape their foes,
The pail kick down; a piteous current flows.

Is't not enough that plagues like these molest?
Must still another foe annoy their rest?
He comes, the pest and terror of the yard,
His full-fledged progeny's imperious guard;
The gander;—spiteful, insolent, and bold,
At the colt's footlock takes his daring hold:
There, serpent-like, escapes a dreadful blow;
And straight attacks a poor defenceless cow:
Each booby goose th' unworthy strife enjoys,
And hails his prowess with redoubled noise.
Then back he stalks, of self-importance full,
Seizes the shaggy foretop of the bull,
Till whirl'd aloft he falls: a timely check,
Enough to dislocate his worthless neck:
For lo! of old, he boasts an honour'd wound;
Behold that broken wing that trails the ground!
Thus fools and bravoes kindred pranks pursue;
As savage quite, and oft as fatal too.
Happy the man that foils an envious elf,
Using the darts of spleen to serve himself.
As when by turns the strolling swine engage

The utmost efforts of the bully's rage,
Whose nibbling warfare on the grunter's side
Is welcome pleasure to his bristly hide ;
Gently he stoops, or, stretch'd at ease along,
Enjoys the insults of the gabbling throng,
That march exulting round his fallen head,
As human victors trample on their dead.

Still Twilight, welcome ! Rest, how sweet art thou !
Now eve o'erhangs the western cloud's thick brow :
The far-stretch'd curtain of retiring light,
With fiery treasures fraught ; that on the sight
Flash from its bulging sides, where darkness lours,
In Fancy's eye, a chain of mould'ring tow'rs ;

Or craggy coasts just rising into view,
Midst jav'lins dire, and darts of streaming blue.

Anon tired labourers bless their shelt'ring home,
When Midnight and the frightful Tempest come.
The Farmer wakes, and sees, with silent dread,
The angry shafts of Heaven gleam round his bed;
The bursting cloud reiterated roars,
Shakes his straw roof, and jars his bolting doors :
The slow-wing'd storm along the troubled skies
Spreads its dark course; the wind begins to rise;
And full-leaf'd elms, his dwelling's shade by day,
With mimic thunder give its fury way :
Sounds in his chimney-top a doleful peal
'Midst pouring rain, or gusts of rattling hail ;
With tenfold danger low the tempest bends,
And quick and strong the sulph'rous flame descends :
The frighten'd mastiff from his kennel flies,
And cringes at the door with piteous cries.—

Where now's the trifler? where the child of pride?
These are the moments when the heart is tried !
Nor lives the man, with conscience e'er so clear,
But feels a solemn, reverential fear ;
Feels too a joy relieve his aching breast,
When the spent storm hath howl'd itself to rest.
Still, welcome beats the long-continued show'r,
And, sleep protracted, comes with double pow'r ;
Calm dreams of bliss bring on the morning sun,
For every barn is fill'd, and Harvest done !

Now, ere sweet Summer bids its long adieu,
And winds blow keen where late the blossom grew,
The bustling day and jovial night must come,
The long-accustom'd feast of Harvest-Home.
No blood-stain'd victory in story bright,

Can give the philosophic mind delight;
No triumph please, while rage and death destroy:
Reflection sickens at the monstrous joy.
And where the joy, if rightly understood,
Like cheerful praise for universal good?

The soul nor check nor doubtful anguish knows,
But free and pure the grateful current flows.

Behold the sound oak table's massy frame
Bestride the kitchen floor! the careful dame

And gen'rous host invite their friends around,
For all that clear'd the crop, or till'd the ground,
Are guests by right of custom :—old and young ;
And many a neighbouring yeoman join the throng,
With artisans that lent their dexterous aid,
When o'er each field the flaming sunbeams play'd.

Yet Plenty reigns, and from her boundless hoard,
Though not one jelly trembles on the board,
Supplies the feast with all that sense can crave ;
With all that made our great forefathers brave,
Ere the cloy'd palate countless flavours tried,
And cooks had Nature's judgment set aside.
With thanks to Heaven, and tales of rustic lore,
The mansion echoes when the banquet's o'er ;
A wider circle spreads, and smiles abound,
As quick the frothing horn performs its round ;
Care's mortal foe ; that sprightly joys imparts
To cheer the frame and elevate their hearts.
Here, fresh and brown, the hazel's produce lies
In tempting heaps, and peals of laughter rise ;
And crackling Music, with the frequent song,
Unheeded bear the midnight hour along.

Here once a year Distinction low'rs its crest :
The master, servant, and the merry guest,
Are equal all ; and round the happy ring
The reaper's eyes exulting glances fling,
And, warm'd with gratitude, he quits his place,
With sunburnt hands and ale-enliven'd face,
Refills the jug his honour'd host to tend,
To serve at once the master and the friend ;
Proud thus to meet his smiles, to share his tale,
His nuts, his conversation, and his ale.

Such were the days,—of days long past I sing,
When Pride gave place to mirth without a sting ;

Ere tyrant customs strength sufficient bore
To violate the feelings of the poor ;
To leave them distanced in the madd'ning race,

Where'er refinement shows its hated face :
Nor causeless hated ;—'t is the peasant's curse,
That hourly makes his wretched station worse ;.

Destroys life's intercourse ; the social plan
That rank to rank cements, as man to man :
Wealth flows around him, Fashion lordly reigns ;
Yet poverty is his, and mental pains.

   Methinks I hear the mourner thus impart
The stifled murmurs of his wounded heart :
" Whence comes this change, ungracious, irksome, cold
Whence the new grandeur that mine eyes behold ?
The widening distance which I daily see,
Has Wealth done this ?—then Wealth's a foe to me :
Foe to our rights ; that leaves a powerful few
The paths of emulation to pursue :—
For emulation stoops to us no more :
The hope of humble industry is o'er ;
The blameless hope, the cheering sweet presage
Of future comforts for declining age.
Can my sons share from this paternal hand
The profits with the labours of the land ?
No ; though indulgent Heaven its blessing deigns,
Where's the small farm to suit my scanty means ?
Content, the Poet sings, with us resides ;
In lonely cots like mine, the damsel hides ;
And will he then in raptur'd visions tell
That sweet Content with Want can never dwell ?
A barley loaf, 'tis true, my table crowns,
That, fast diminishing in lusty rounds,
Stops Nature's cravings ; yet her sighs will flow
From knowing this,—that once it was not so.
Our annual feast, when Earth her plenty yields,
When crown'd with boughs the last load quits the fields,
The aspect still of ancient joy puts on ;
The aspect only, with the substance gone :
The self-same horn is still at our command,
But serves none now but the plebeian hand :
For home-brew'd ale, neglected and debas'd,

Is quite discarded from the realms of taste.
Where unaffected Freedom charm'd the soul,
The separate table and the costly bowl,
Cool as the blast that checks the budding Spring,
A mockery of gladness round them fling.
For oft the Farmer, ere his heart approves,
Yields up the custom which he dearly loves :
Refinement forces on him like a tide ;
Bold innovations down its current ride,
That bear no peace beneath their showy dress,
Nor add one tittle to his happiness.
His guests selected, rank's punctilios known ;
What trouble waits upon a casual frown !
Restraint's foul manacles his pleasures maim ;
Selected guests selected phrases claim :
Nor reigns that joy, when hand in hand they join,
That good old Master felt in shaking mine.
Heaven bless his memory ! bless his honoured name !
(The poor will speak his lasting worthy fame :)
To soul's fair-purpos'd strength and guidance give ;
In pity to us still let goodness live :
Let labour have its due ! my cot shall be
From chilling want and guilty murmurs free.
Let labour have its due ; then peace is mine,
And never, never shall my heart repine."

AUTUMN.

ACORNS—HOGS IN THE WOOD—WHEAT SOWING—THE CHURCH—VILLAGE GIRLS
—THE MAD GIRL—THE BIRD BOY'S HUT—DISAPPOINTMENT; REFLECTIONS,
ETC.—EUSTON-HALL—FOX-HUNTING—OLD TROUNCER—LONG NIGHTS—A
WELCOME TO WINTER.

AGAIN, the year's decline, 'midst storms and floods,
The thund'ring chase, the yellow fading woods,
Invite my song; that fain would boldly tell
Of upland coverts, and the echoing dell.

By turns resounding loud, at eve and morn,
The swineherd's halloo, or the huntsman's horn.

No more the fields with scatter'd grain supply
The restless wandering tenants of the sty;.
From oak to oak they run with eager haste,
And wrangling share the first delicious taste
Of fallen acorns ; yet but thinly found
Till the strong gale has shook them to the ground.
It comes ; and roaring woods obedient wave :
Their home well pleas'd the joint adventurers leave :
The trudging sow leads forth her numerous young,
Playful, and white, and clean, the briars among,
Till briars and thorns increasing fence them round,
Where last year's smould'ring leaves bestrew the ground,
And o'er their heads, loud lash'd by furious squalls,
Bright from their cups the rattling treasure falls ;
Hot, thirsty food ; whence doubly sweet and cool
The welcome margin of some rush-grown pool,
The wild duck's lonely haunt, whose jealous eye
Guards every point ; who sits, prepar'd to fly,
On the calm bosom of her little lake,
Too closely screen'd for ruffian winds to shake ;
And as the bold intruders press around,
At once she starts, and rises with a bound :
With bristles rais'd the sudden noise they hear,
And ludicrously wild, and wing'd with fear,
The herd decamp with more than swinish speed,
And snorting dash through sedge, and rush, and reed :
Through tangling thickets headlong on they go,
Then stop and listen for their fancied foe ;
The hindmost still the growing panic spreads,
Repeated fright the first alarm succeeds,
Till Folly's wages, wounds and thorns, they reap :
Yet glorying in their fortunate escape,
Their groundless terrors by degrees soon cease,

And Night's dark reign restores their wonted peace.
For now the gale subsides, and from each bough
The roosting pheasant's short but frequent crow
Invites to rest; and, huddling side by side,
The herd in closest ambush seek to hide;

Seek some warm slope with shagged moss o'erspread,
Dried leaves their copious covering and their bed:
In vain may Giles, through gath'ring glooms that fall,
And solemn silence, urge his piercing call:

Whole days and nights they tarry 'midst their store,
Nor quit the woods till oaks can yield no more.

Beyond bleak Winter's rage, beyond the Spring
That rolling earth's unvarying course will bring,
Who tills the ground looks on with mental eye,
And sees next Summer's sheaves and cloudless sky;
And even now, whilst Nature's beauty dies,
Deposits seed, and bids new harvests rise;
Seed well prepared, and warm'd with glowing lime,
'Gainst earth-bred grubs, and cold, and lapse of time:
For searching frosts and various ills invade,
Whilst wintry months depress the springing blade.
The plough moves heavily, and strong the soil,
And clogging harrows with augmented toil
Dive deep: and clinging, mixes with the mould
A fatt'ning treasure from the nightly fold,
And all the cow-yard's highly valued store,
That late bestrew'd the blacken'd surface o'er.
No idling hours are here, when Fancy trims
Her dancing taper over outstretch'd limbs,
And, in her thousand thousand colours drest,
Plays round the grassy couch of noontide rest:
Here Giles for hours of indolence atones
With strong exertion, and with weary bones,
And knows no leisure; till the distant chime
Of Sabbath bells he hears at sermon time,
That down the brook sound sweetly in the gale,
Or strike the rising hill, or skim the dale.

Nor his alone the sweets of ease to taste:
Kind rest extends to all :—save one poor beast,
That, true to time and pace, is doom'd to plod,
To bring the Pastor to the House of God:
Mean structure; where no bones of heroes lie!
The rude inelegance of poverty

Reigns here alone : else why that roof of straw ?
Those narrow windows with the frequent flaw ?
O'er whose low cells the dock and mallow spread,
And rampant nettles lift the spiry head,
Whilst from the hollows of the tower on high
The grey-capp'd daws in saucy legions fly.

Round these lone walls assembling neighbours meet,
And tread departed friends beneath their feet ;
And new-briar'd graves, that prompt the secret sigh,
Show each the spot where he himself must lie.

'Midst timely greetings village news goes round,
Of crops late shorn, or crops that deck the ground;
Experienced ploughmen in the circle join;
While sturdy boys, in feats of strength to shine,
With pride elate, their young associates brave
To jump from hollow-sounding grave to grave;
Then close consulting, each his talent lends
To plan fresh sports when tedious service ends.

Hither at times, with cheerfulness of soul,
Sweet village maids from neighbouring hamlets stroll,
That, like the light-heel'd does o'er lawns that rove,
Look shyly curious; rip'ning into love;
For love's their errand: hence the tints that glow
On either cheek, a heighten'd lustre know:
When, conscious of their charms, e'en Age looks sly,
And rapture beams from Youth's observant eye.

The pride of such a party, Nature's pride,
Was lovely Poll; who innocently tried,
With hat of airy shape and ribbons gay,
Love to inspire, and stand in Hymen's way:
But, ere her twentieth summer could expand,
Or youth was render'd happy with her hand,
Her mind's serenity, her peace was gone,
Her eye grew languid, and she wept alone:
Yet causeless seem'd her grief; for quick restrain'd,
Mirth follow'd loud; or indignation reign'd:
Whims wild and simple led her from her home,
The heath, the common, or the fields to roam:
Terror and joy alternate ruled her hours;
Now blithe she sung, and gather'd useless flow'rs;
Now pluck'd a tender twig from every bough,
To whip the hov'ring demons from her brow.
Ill-fated maid! thy guiding spark is fled,
And lasting wretchedness awaits thy bed—

Thy bed of straw! for mark, where even now
O'er their lost child afflicted parents bow;
Their woe she knows not, but perversely coy,

Inverted customs yield her sullen joy!
Her midnight meals in secrecy she takes,
Low mutt'ring to the moon, that rising breaks

Thro' night's dark gloom :—oh, how much more forlorn
Her night, that knows of no returning morn !—
Slow from the threshold, once her infant seat,
O'er the cold earth she crawls to her retreat ;
Quitting the cot's warm walls, unhoused to lie,
Or share the swine's impure and narrow sty ;
The damp night air her shiv'ring limbs assails :
In dreams she moans, and fancied wrongs bewails.
When morning wakes, none earlier roused than she,
When pendent drops fall glitt'ring from the tree ;
But nought her rayless melancholy cheers,
Or soothes her breast, or stops her streaming tears.
Her matted locks unornamented flow ;
Clasping her knees, and waving to and fro ;—
Her head bow'd down, her faded cheek to hide ;—
A piteous mourner by the pathway side.
Some tufted molehill through the livelong day
She calls her throne : there weeps her life away :
And oft the gaily passing stranger stays
His well-timed step, and takes a silent gaze,
Till sympathetic drops unbidden start,
And pangs quick springing muster round his heart ;
And soft he treads with other gazers round,
And fain would catch her sorrow's plaintive sound.
One word alone is all that strikes the ear,
One short, pathetic, simple word,—" Oh dear !"
A thousand times repeated to the wind,
That wafts the sigh, but leaves the pang behind !
For ever of the proffer'd parley shy,
She hears th' unwelcome foot advancing nigh ;
Nor quite unconscious of her wretched plight,
Gives one sad look and hurries out of sight.—

Fair promised sunbeams of terrestrial bliss,
Health's gallant hopes,—and are ye sunk to this ?
For in life's road, though thorns abundant grow,

There still are joys poor Poll can never know;
Joys which the gay companions of her prime
Sip as they drift along the stream of time:
At eve to hear beside their tranquil home
The lifted latch, that speaks the lover come:
That love matured, next playful on the knee
To press the velvet lip of infancy;
To stay the tottering step, the features trace;—
Inestimable sweets of social peace!

O Thou, who bidd'st the vernal juices rise!
Thou, on whose blasts autumnal foliage flies!
Let Peace ne'er leave me, nor my heart grow cold,
Whilst life and sanity are mine to hold.

Shorn of their flow'rs that shed th' untreasured seed,
The withering pasture, and the fading mead,
Less tempting grown, diminish more and more,
The dairy's pride; sweet Summer's flowing store.
New cares succeed, and gentle duties press,
Where the fire-side, a school of tenderness,
Revives the languid chirp, and warms the blood
Of cold-nipp'd weaklings of the latter brood,
That from the shell just bursting into day,
Through yard or pond pursue their vent'rous way.

Far weightier cares and wider scenes expand;
What devastation marks the new-sown land!
"From hungry woodland's foes go, Giles, and guard
The rising wheat, ensure its great reward:
A future sustenance, a Summer's pride,
Demand thy vigilance: then be it tried:
Exert thy voice, and wield thy shotless gun:
Go, tarry there from morn till setting sun."

Keen blows the blast, or ceaseless rain descends;
The half-stripp'd hedge a sorry shelter lends.

Oh for a hovel, e'er so small or low,
Whose roof, repelling winds and early snow,
Might bring home's comforts fresh before his eyes!
No sooner thought, than see the structure rise,
In some sequester'd nook, embank'd around,

Sods for its walls, and straw in burdens bound!
Dried fuel hoarded is his richest store,
And circling smoke obscures his little door :
Whence creeping forth, to duty's call he yields,
And strolls the Crusoe of the lonely fields.

On whitethorns tow'ring, and the leafless rose,
A frost-nipt feast in bright vermilion glows ;
Where clust'ring sloes in glossy order rise,
He crops the loaded branch ; a cumbrous prize :
And o'er the flame the splutt'ring fruit he rests,
Placing green sods to seat the coming guests ;
His guests by promise ; playmates young and gay :—
But ah ! fresh pastimes lure their steps away !
He sweeps his hearth, and homeward looks in vain,
Till, feeling Disappointment's cruel pain,
His fairy revels are exchanged for rage,
His banquet marr'd, grown dull his hermitage.
The field becomes his prison, till on high
Benighted birds to shades and coverts fly.
'Midst air, health, daylight, can he prisoner be ?
If fields are prisons, where is Liberty ?
Here still she dwells, and here her votaries stroll ;
But disappointed hope untunes the soul :
Restraints unfelt whilst hours of rapture flow,
When troubles press, to chains and barriers grow.
Look then from trivial up to greater woes ;
From the poor bird-boy with his roasted sloes,
To where the dungeon'd mourner heaves the sigh,
Where not one cheering sunbeam meets his eye.
Though ineffectual pity thine may be,
No wealth, no pow'r, to set the captive free ;
Though only to thy ravish'd sight is given
The radiant path that Howard trod to heaven ;
Thy slights can make the wretched more forlorn,
And deeper drive affliction's barbed thorn.
Say not, " I'll come and cheer thy gloomy cell
With news of dearest friends ; how good, how well :
I'll be a joyful herald to thine heart ;"
Then fail, and play the worthless trifler's part,
To sip flat pleasures from thy glass's brim,
And waste the precious hour that's due to him.

In mercy spare the base, unmanly blow :
Where can he turn, to whom complain of you ?
Back to past joys in vain his thoughts may stray,
Trace and retrace the beaten, worn-out way,
The rankling injury will pierce his breast,
And curses on thee break his midnight rest.

Bereft of song, and ever-cheering green,
The soft endearments of the Summer scene,
New harmony pervades the solemn wood,
Dear to the soul, and healthful to the blood :
For bold exertion follows on the sound
Of distant sportsmen, and the chiding hound ;
First heard from kennel bursting, mad with joy,
Where smiling Euston boasts her good Fitzroy,
Lord of pure alms, and gifts that wide extend ;
The farmer's patron, and the poor man's friend :
Whose mansion glitters with the eastern ray,
Whose elevated temple points the way,
O'er slopes and lawns, the park's extensive pride,
To where the victims of the chase reside,
Ingulf'd in earth, in conscious safety warm,
Till lo ! a plot portends their coming harm.

In earliest hours of dark and hooded morn,
Ere yet one rosy cloud bespeaks the dawn,
Whilst far abroad the Fox pursues his prey,
He's doom'd to risk the perils of the day,
From his stronghold block'd out ; perhaps to bleed,
Or owe his life to fortune or to speed.
For now the pack, impatient rushing on,
Range through the darkest coverts one by one ;
Trace every spot ; whilst down each noble glade
That guides the eye beneath a changeful shade,
The loit'ring sportsman feels th' instinctive flame,
And checks his steed to mark the springing game.

'Midst intersecting cuts and winding ways
The huntsman cheers his dogs, and anxious strays
Where every narrow riding, even shorn,
Gives back the echo of his mellow horn :
Till fresh and lightsome, every pow'r untried,

The starting fugitive leaps by his side,
His lifted finger to his ear he plies,
And the view-halloo bids a chorus rise
Of dogs quick-mouth'd, and shouts that mingle loud
As bursting thunder rolls from cloud to cloud.

With ears erect, and chest of vig'rous mould,
O'er ditch, o'er fence, unconquerably bold,
The shining courser lengthens every bound,
And his strong foot-locks suck the moisten'd ground,
As from the confines of the wood they pour,
And joyous villages partake the roar.
O'er heath far-stretch'd, or down, or valley low,
The stiff-limb'd peasant, glorying in the show,
Pursues in vain; where Youth itself soon tires,
Spite of the transports that the chase inspires;
For who unmounted long can charm the eye,
Or hear the music of the leading cry?

Poor faithful Trouncer! thou canst lead no more;
All thy fatigues and all thy triumphs o'er!
Triumphs of worth, whose long-excelling fame
Was still to follow true the hunted game!
Beneath enormous oaks, Britannia's boast,
In thick, impenetrable coverts lost,
When the warm pack in faltering silence stood,
Thine was the note that roused the list'ning wood,
Rekindling every joy with tenfold force,
Through all the mazes of the tainted course.
Still foremost thou the dashing stream to cross,
And tempt along the animated horse;
Foremost o'er fen or level mead to pass,
And sweep the show'ring dew-drops from the grass;
Then bright emerging from the mist below,
To climb the woodland hill's exulting brow.

Pride of thy race! with worth far less than thine,
Full many human leaders daily shine!
Less faith, less constancy, less gen'rous zeal!—
Then no disgrace my humble verse shall feel,
Where not one lying line to riches bows,
Or poison'd sentiments from rancour flows;

H

Nor flowers are strewn around Ambition's car :
An honest dog's a nobler theme by far.
Each sportsman heard the tidings with a sigh,
When Death's cold touch had stopt his tuneful cry ;
And though high deeds, and fair exalted praise,
In memory liv'd, and flow'd in rustic lays,

Short was the strain of monumental woe :
" *Foxes, rejoice ! here buried lies your foe.*"
In safety housed, throughout Night's length'ning reign,
The cock sends forth a loud and piercing strain ;
More frequent, as the glooms of midnight flee,
And hours roll round, that brought him liberty,

When Summer's early dawn, mild, clear, and bright,
Chased quick away the transitory night :—
Hours now in darkness veil'd ; yet loud the scream
Of geese impatient for the playful stream ;
And all the feather'd tribe imprison'd raise
Their morning notes of inharmonious praise ;
And many a clamorous hen and cock rel gay,
When daylight slowly through the fog breaks way,
Fly wantonly abroad : but, ah, how soon
The shades of twilight follow hazy noon,
Short'ning the busy day !—day that slides by
Amidst th' unfinish'd toils of husbandry ;
Toils still each morn resumed with double care
To meet the icy terrors of the year ;
To meet the threats of Boreas undismay'd,
And Winter's gathering frowns and hoary head.

Then welcome, Cold ; welcome, ye snowy nights !
Heaven 'midst your rage shall mingle pure delights,
And confidence of hope the soul sustain,
While devastation sweeps along the plain :
Nor shall the child of poverty despair,
But bless the Power that rules the changing year ;
Assured,—though horrors round his cottage reign,—
That Spring will come, and Nature smile again.

WINTER.

TENDERNESS TO CATTLE—FROZEN TURNIPS—THE COW-YARD—NIGHT—THE
FARM-HOUSE—FIRE-SIDE—FARMER'S ADVICE AND INSTRUCTION—NIGHTLY
CARES OF THE STABLE—DOBBIN—THE POST-HORSE—SHEEP-STEALING DOGS
—WALKS OCCASIONED THEREBY—THE GHOST—LAMB TIME—RETURNING
SPRING—CONCLUSION.

WITH kindred pleasures moved, and cares opprest,
Sharing alike our weariness and rest;

Who lives the daily partner of our hours,
Through every change of heat, and frost, and showers,
Partakes our cheerful meals, partaking first
In mutual labour, and fatigue, and thirst ;
The, kindly intercourse will ever prove
A bond of amity and social love.
To more than man this generous warmth extends,
And oft the team and shiv'ring herd befriends ;
Tender solicitude the bosom fills,
And pity executes what reason wills :
Youth learns compassion's tale from every tongue,
And flies to aid the helpless and the young.

When now, unsparing as the scourge of war,
Blasts follow blasts, and groves dismantled roar,
Around their home the storm-pinch'd cattle lows,
No nourishment in frozen pastures grows ;
Yet frozen pastures every morn resound
With fair abundance thund'ring to the ground.
For though on hoary twigs no buds peep out,
And e'en the hardy brambles cease to sprout,
Beneath dread Winter's level sheets of snow
The sweet nutritious Turnip deigns to grow.
Till now imperious Want and wide-spread Dearth
Bid Labour claim her treasures from the earth.
On Giles, and such as Giles, the labour falls,
To strew the frequent load where hunger calls.
On driving gales sharp hail indignant flies,
And sleet, more irksome still, assails his eyes ;
Snow clogs his feet ; or if no snow is seen,
The field with all its juicy store to screen,
Deep goes the frost, till every root is found
A rolling mass of ice upon the ground.
No tender ewe can break her nightly fast,
Nor heifer strong begin the cold repast,
Till Giles with ponderous beetle foremost go,
And scattering splinters fly at every blow ;

When pressing round him, eager for the prize,
From their mixt breath warm exhalations rise.

In beaded rows if drops now deck the spray,
While the sun grants a momentary ray,
Let but a cloud's broad shadow intervene,
And stiffen'd into gems the drops are seen ;
And down the furrow'd oak's broad southern side
Streams of dissolving rime no longer glide.

Though Night approaching bids for rest prepare,
Still the flail echoes through the frosty air,
Nor stops till deepest shades of darkness come,
Sending at length the weary labourer home.
From him, with bed and nightly food supplied,
Throughout the yard, housed round on every side,
Deep-plunging cows their rustling feast enjoy,
And snatch sweet mouthfuls from the passing boy,
Who moves unseen beneath his trailing load,
Fills the tall racks, and leaves a scatter'd road ;
Where oft the swine from ambush warm and dry
Bolt out, and scamper headlong to their sty,
When Giles with well-known voice, already there,
Deigns them a portion of his evening care.

Him, though the cold may pierce, and storms molest,
Succeeding hours shall cheer with warmth and rest ;
Gladness to spread, and raise the grateful smile,
He hurls the faggot bursting from the pile,
And many a log and rifted trunk conveys,
To heap the fire, and wide extend the blaze,
That quivering strong through every opening flies,
Whilst smoky columns unobstructed rise.
For the rude architect, unknown to fame,
(Nor symmetry nor elegance his aim,)
Who spread his floors of solid oak on high,
On beams rough hewn, from age to age that lie,

Bade his wide- fabric unimpair'd sustain
The orchard's store, and cheese, and golden grain ;
Bade from its central base, capacious laid,

The well-wrought chimney rear its lofty head ;
Where since hath many a savoury ham been stored,
And tempests howl'd and Christmas gambols roar'd.

Flat on the hearth the glowing embers lie,
And flames reflected dance in every eye :
There the long billet, forced at last to bend,
While gushing sap froths out at either end,
Throws round its welcome heat :—the ploughman smiles,
And oft the joke runs hard on sheepish Giles,
Who sits joint tenant of the corner-stool,
The converse sharing, though in duty's school ;
For now attentively 'tis his to hear
Interrogations from the Master's chair.

"Left ye your bleating charge, when daylight fled,
Near where the hay-stack lifts its snowy head ?
Whose fence of bushy furze, so close and warm,
May stop the slanting bullets of the storm.
For, hark ! it blows ; a dark and dismal night :
Heaven guide the traveller's fearful steps aright !
Now from the woods, mistrustful, and sharp-eyed,
The fox in silent darkness seems to glide,
Stealing around us, listening as he goes,
If chance the cock or stammering capon crows,
Or goose, or nodding duck, should darkling cry,
As if apprised of lurking danger nigh :
Destruction waits them, Giles, if e'er you fail
To bolt their doors against the driving gale.
Strew'd you (still mindful of th' unshelter'd head)
Burdens of straw, the cattle's welcome bed ?
Thine heart should feel, what thou mayst hourly see,
That *duty's basis is humanity.*
Of pain's unsavoury cup though thou mayst taste
(The wrath of Winter from the bleak north-east),
Thine utmost suff'rings in the coldest day
A period terminates, and joys repay.
Perhaps e'en now, while here those joys we boast,
Full many a bark rides down the neighb'ring coast,
Where the high northern waves tremendous roar,
Drove down by blasts from Norway's icy shore.

The sea-boy there, less fortunate than thou,
Feels all thy pains in all the gusts that blow;
His freezing hands now drench'd, now dry, by turns;
Now lost, now seen, the distant light that burns,
On some tall cliff upraised, a flaming guide,

That throws its friendly radiance o'er the tide.
His labours cease not with declining day,
But toils and perils mark his wat'ry way;
And whilst in peaceful dreams secure we lie,
The ruthless whirlwinds rage along the sky,

I

Round his head whistling;—and shalt thou repine,
While this protecting roof still shelters thine?"

Mild as the vernal show'r, his words prevail,
And aid the moral precept of his tale:
His wond'ring hearers learn, and ever keep
These first ideas of the restless deep:
And, as the opening mind a circuit tries,
Present felicities in value rise.
Increasing pleasures every hour they find,
The warmth more precious, and the shelter kind;
Warmth that long reigning bids the eyelids close,
As through the blood its balmy influence goes,
When the cheer'd heart forgets fatigues and cares,
And drowsiness alone dominion bears.

Sweet then the Ploughman's slumbers, hale and young,
When the last topic dies upon his tongue;
Sweet then the bliss his transient dreams inspire,
Till chilblains wake him, or the snapping fire:
He starts, and ever thoughtful of his team,
Along the glitt'ring snow a feeble gleam
Shoots from his lantern, as he yawning goes
To add fresh comforts to their night's repose;
Diffusing fragrance as their food he moves,
And pats the jolly sides of those he loves.
Thus full replenish'd, perfect ease possest,
From night till morn alternate food and rest,
No rightful cheer withheld, no sleep debarr'd,
Their each day's labour brings its sure reward.
Yet when from plough or lumb'ring cart set free,
They taste awhile the sweets of liberty:
E'en sober Dobbin lifts his clumsy heel
And kicks, disdainful of the dirty wheel;
But soon, his frolic ended, yields again
To trudge the road, and wear the clinking chain.

Short-sighted Dobbin !—thou canst only see
The trivial hardships that encompass thee :
Thy chains were freedom, and thy toils repose,
Could the poor post-horse tell thee all his woes,

Show thee his bleeding shoulders, and unfold
The dreadful anguish he endures for gold :
Hired at each call of business, lust, or rage,
That prompts the trav'ller on from stage to stage.

Still on his strength depends their boasted speed;
For them his limbs grow weak, his bare ribs bleed;
And though he groaning quickens at command,
Their extra shilling in the rider's hand
Becomes his bitter scourge,—'t is he must feel
The double efforts of the lash and steel;
Till when, up hill, the destined hill he gains,
And trembling under complicated pains,
Prone from his nostrils, darting on the ground,
His breath emitted floats in clouds around:
Drops chase each other down his chest and sides,
And spatter'd mud his native colour hides:
Through his swoln veins the boiling torrent flows,
And every nerve a separate torture knows.
His harness loosed, he welcomes, eager-eyed,
The pail's full draught that quivers by his side;
And joys to see the well-known stable-door,
As the starved mariner the friendly shore.

Ah, well for him if here his sufferings ceased,
And ample hours of rest his pains appeased!
But roused again, and sternly bade to rise,
And shake refreshing slumber from his eyes,
Ere his exhausted spirits can return,
Or through his frame reviving ardour burn,
Come forth he must, though limping, maim'd, and sore;
He hears the whip; the chaise is at the door:—
The collar tightens, and again he feels
His half-heal'd wounds inflamed; again the wheels
With tiresome sameness in his ears resound,
O'er blinding dust, or miles of flinty ground.
Thus nightly robb'd and injured day by day,
His piecemeal murderers wear his life away.
What say'st thou, Dobbin? what though hounds await
With open jaws the moment of thy fate,
No better fate attends his public race;
His life is misery, and his end disgrace.

Then freely bear thy burden to the mill;
Obey but one short law,—thy driver's will.
Affection to thy memory ever true,
Shall boast of mighty loads that Dobbin drew;
And back to childhood shall the mind with pride
Recount thy gentleness in many a ride
To pond, or field, or village fair, when thou
Held'st high thy braided mane and comely brow;
And oft the tale shall rise to homely fame
Upon thy gen'rous spirit and thy name.

    Though faithful to a proverb we regard
The midnight Chieftain of the farmer's yard,
Beneath whose guardianship all hearts rejoice,
Woke by the echo of his hollow voice;
Yet as the hound may falt'ring quit the pack,
Snuff the foul scent and hasten yelping back;
And e'en the docile pointer know disgrace,
Thwarting the general instinct of his race;
E'en so the mastiff, or the meaner cur,
At times will from the path of duty err,
(A pattern of fidelity by day,
By night a murderer, lurking for his prey,)
And round the pastures or the fold will creep,
And, coward-like, attack the peaceful sheep.
Alone the wanton mischief he pursues,
Alone in reeking blood his jaws imbrues;
Chasing amain his frighten'd victims round,
Till death in wild confusion strews the ground;
Then wearied out, to kennel sneaks away,
And licks his guilty paws till break of day.

    The deed discover'd, and the news once spread,
Vengeance hangs o'er the unknown culprit's head:
And careful Shepherds extra hours bestow
In patient watchings for the common foe

A foe most dreaded now, when rest and peace
Should wait the season of the flock's increase.

In part these nightly terrors to dispel,
Giles, ere he sleeps, his little flock must tell.

From the fire-side with many a shrug he hies,
Glad if the full-orb'd moon salute his eyes,
And through th' unbroken stillness of the night
Shed on his path her beams of cheering light.

With saunt'ring step he climbs the distant stile,
Whilst all around him wears a placid smile;
There views the white-robed clouds in clusters driven,
And all the glorious pageantry of heaven.
Low, on the utmost boundary of the sight,
The rising vapours catch the silver light;
Thence Fancy measures, as they parting fly,
Which first will throw its shadow on the eye,
Passing the source of light; and thence away,
Succeeded quick by brighter still than they.
Far yet above these wafted clouds are seen
(In a remoter sky, still more serene)
Others, detach'd in ranges through the air,
Spotless as snow, and countless as they're fair;
Scatter'd immensely wide from east to west,
The beauteous 'semblance of a flock at rest.
These, to the raptured mind, aloud proclaim
Their Mighty Shepherd's everlasting name.

Whilst thus the loiterer's. utmost stretch of soul
Climbs the still clouds, or passes those that roll,
And loosed Imagination soaring goes
High o'er his home, and all his little woes,
Time glides away; neglected duty calls;
At once from plains of light to earth he falls,
And down a narrow lane, well known by day,
With all his speed pursues his sounding way,
In thought still half absorb'd and chill'd with cold
When lo! an object frightful to behold;
A grisly Spectre, cloth'd in silver-grey,
Around whose feet the waving shadows play,
Stands in his path!—He stops, and not a breath
Heaves from his heart, that sinks almost to death.
Loud the owl halloos o'er his head unseen;
All else is silent, dismally serene:
Some prompt ejaculation, whisper'd low,
Yet bears him up against the threat'ning foe;

And thus poor Giles, though half inclined to fly,
Mutters his doubts, and strains his steadfast eye.
" 'Tis not my crimes thou com'st here to reprove;
No murders stain my soul, no perjured love;
If thou 'rt indeed what here thou seem'st to be,
Thy dreadful mission cannot reach to me.
By parents taught still to mistrust mine eyes,
Still to approach each object of surprise,
Lest Fancy's formful visions should deceive
In moonlight paths, or glooms of falling eve,
This then's the moment when my mind should try
To scan thy motionless deformity;
But oh, the fearful task! yet well I know
An aged ash, with many a spreading bough,
(Beneath whose leaves I've found a Summer's bower,
Beneath whose trunk I've weather'd many a shower,)
Stands singly down this solitary way,
But far beyond where now my footsteps stay.
'Tis true, thus far I've come with heedless haste;
No reck'ning kept, no passing objects traced :—
And can I then have reach'd that very tree?
Or is its reverend form assumed by thee?"
The happy thought alleviates his pain :
He creeps another step; then stops again;
Till slowly, as his noiseless feet draw near,
Its perfect lineaments at once appear;
Its crown of shivering ivy whispering peace,
And its white bark that fronts the moon's pale face.
Now, whilst his blood mounts upward, now he knows
The solid gain that from conviction flows;
And strengthen'd Confidence shall hence fulfil
(With conscious Innocence more valued still)
The dreariest task that winter nights can bring,
By churchyard dark, or grove or fairy ring;
Still buoying up the timid mind of youth,
Till loit'ring Reason hoists the scale of Truth.
With these blest guardians Giles his course pursues,

Till numbering his heavy-sided ewes,
Surrounding stillness tranquillize his breast,
And shape the dreams that wait his hours of rest.

As when retreating tempests we behold,
Whose skirts at length the azure sky unfold,
And full of murmurings and mingled wrath,
Slowly unshroud the smiling face of earth,

Bringing the bosom joy: so Winter flies!—
And see the source of life and light uprise!
A height'ning arch o'er southern hills he bends,
Warm on the cheek the slanting beam descends,
And gives the reeking mead a brighter hue,
And draws the modest primrose bud to view.
Yet frosts succeed, and winds impetuous rush,
And hail-storms rattle through the budding bush;
And night-fall'n lambs require the shepherd's care,
And teeming ewes, that still their burdens bear;
Beneath whose sides to-morrow's dawn may see
The milk-white strangers bow the trembling knee;
At whose first birth the powerful instinct's seen
That fills with champions the daisied green :
For Ewes that stood aloof with fearful eye,
With stamping foot now men and dogs defy,
And, obstinately faithful to their young,
Guard their first steps to join the bleating throng.

But casualties and death from damps and cold
Will still attend the well-conducted fold :
Her tender offspring dead, the dam aloud
Calls, and runs wild amidst th' unconscious crowd :
And orphan'd sucklings raise the piteous cry;
No wool to warm them, no defenders nigh.
And must her streaming milk then flow in vain?
Must unregarded innocence complain?
No;—ere this strong solicitude subside,
Maternal fondness may be fresh applied,
And the adopted stripling still may find
A parent most assiduously kind.
For this he's doomed awhile disguised to range
(For fraud or force must work the wish'd-for change);
For this his predecessor's skin he wears,
Till, cheated into tenderness and cares,
The unsuspecting dam, contented grown,
Cherish and guard the fondlings as her own.

Thus all by turns to fair perfection rise ;
Thus twins are parted to increase their size :
Thus instinct yields as interest points the way,
Till the bright flock, augmenting every day,
On sunny hills and vales of springing flowers
With ceaseless clamour greet the vernal hours.

The humbler Shepherd here with joy beholds
Th' approved economy of crowded folds,
And, in his small contracted round of cares,
Adjusts the practice of each hint he hears ;
For boys with emulation learn to glow,
And boast their pastures, and their healthful show

Of well-grown lambs, the glory of the spring ;
And field to field in competition bring.

E'en Giles, for all his cares and watchings past,
And all his contests with the wintry blast,
Claims a full share of that sweet praise bestow'd
By gazing neighbours, when along the road,
Or village green, his curly-coated throng
Suspends the chorus of the spinner's song ;
When Admiration's unaffected grace
Lisps from the tongue, and beams in ev'ry face :
Delightful moments !—Sunshine, Health, and Joy
Play round, and cheer the elevated boy !
" Another Spring ! " his heart exulting cries ;
" Another Year ! " with promised blessings rise !—
" Eternal Power ! from whom those blessings flow,
Teach me still more to wonder, more to know :
Seed-time and Harvest let me see again ;
Wander the leaf-strewn wood, the frozen plain :
Let the first flower, corn-waving field, plain, tree,
Here round my home still lift my soul to Thee ;
And let me ever, 'midst thy bounties, raise
An humble note of thankfulness and praise ! "

THE END.